Other books i[n]
THE TIME WARP TRIO series

# THE TIME WARP TRIO

# Summer Reading Is Killing Me!

## by Jon Scieszka

### illustrated by Lane Smith

SCHOLASTIC INC.
New York Toronto London Auckland Sydney
Mexico City New Delhi Hong Kong

Grateful acknowledgement is made for permission
to use the following copyrighted characters:
"Horned King" from *The Book of Three*
by Lloyd Alexander (Henry Holt & Co.)
By permission of the author.
"Henrietta Chicken" from *The Hoboken Chicken Emergency*
by Daniel Pinkwater (Atheneum)
By permission of the author.
"Charlotte" from *Charlotte's Web* by E. B. White (HarperCollins).
By permission of the estate of E. B. White.

ISBN 0-439-08330-3

12 11 10 9 8 7 6 5 4 3 2 1            9/9 0 1 2 3 4/0

Printed in the U.S.A.            40

First Scholastic printing, September 1999

Title hand lettered by Michele Laporte.
Set in Sabon.

The characters and events in this book are fictitious. Any similarity to real characters or real events is very interesting. Does this happen to you often?

A special thanks to Lloyd Alexander, Daniel Pinkwater, and the E. B. White estate for allowing their characters to appear in this book. May millions of kids meet the Horned King, Henrietta, and Charlotte, and go find them in their original books.

Dedicated to all of those authors who saved me from getting killed by summer reading:

Aesop, Lloyd Alexander, Natalie Babbitt, Ludwig Bemelmans, Raymond Briggs, Jeff Brown, Eric Carle, Lewis Carroll, John Christopher, Beverly Cleary, Roald Dahl, Daniel Defoe, Marjorie Flack, Esther Forbes, Jean Craighead George, William Golding, Kenneth Grahame, Florence Parry Heide, James Howe, Washington Irving, Crockett Johnson, Ruth Krauss, C. S. Lewis, Astrid Lindgren, Arnold Lobel, Patricia MacLachlan, James Marshall, Robert McCloskey, Herman Melville, A. A. Milne, Peggy Parish, Katherine Paterson, Gary Paulsen, Daniel Manus Pinkwater, Beatrix Potter, H. A. Rey, W. H. D. Rouse, Louis Sachar, Dr. Seuss, Marjorie W. Sharmat, Mary Shelley, Donald J. Sobol, William Steig, Robert Louis Stevenson, Bram Stoker, Rosemary Sutcliff, J. R. R. Tolkien, P. L. Travers, Mark Twain, Jules Verne, E. B. White and Laura Ingalls Wilder.

# ONE

"CLUCK, CLUCK," the thing rumbled in a deep voice.

"Is that thing talking to us?" said Fred.

I looked around the small playground. Fred, Sam, and I stood at one end against a chain-link fence. A very large, white, feathered thing stood next to the swing set at the other end. It had yellow, scaly legs as big as baseball bats, little red eyes, and a dog collar.

"I think it's a giant chicken," I said.

Sam cleaned his glasses on his T-shirt and took another look at the other side of the playground. "Yes, that is a two-hundred-fifty-pound chicken standing there."

The sun glittered in its hungry little eyes.

"And yes, he looks like he's planning to hurt us," added Sam.

"Hey, it's not my fault," said Fred. "I didn't touch *The Book*."

"You did too," I said.

"Did not," said Fred.

"Did too."

"Did not." .

"Did too."

"Excuse me, guys," said Sam. "Did you ever get the feeling that all of this has happened before, exactly like this?"

The super-size chicken eyed us. He gave another gut-rumbling "CLUCK."

"Well, except with maybe a black knight instead of a giant chicken, of course."

Fred pushed back his Red Wings hat and scratched his head. "Hey yeah. It's like 'a la mode' or something."

The chicken pecked the ground hungrily with jackhammer blows of its beak.

"You mean 'déjà vu,'" said Sam, backing up against the fence. "And Joe, isn't this right about when you should do some magic trick and get us out of here?"

I stood there stunned, looking at a giant white chicken on a city playground. The swing set, the

slide, the gravel, even the impossible chicken . . .
Sam was right. Everything did look familiar, but
not really familiar. I couldn't put my finger on it.

"Uh, Joe. *Joe?*" said Sam, elbowing me in the
ribs while keeping his eye on the hungry chicken.
"The magic trick?"

"It's like I've been here before, but I haven't really been here before," I said.

The monster bird twisted its head. It looked us
over with one eye, then the other.

"Well, thank you for sharing your feelings,"
said Sam. "And you know we would
just love to hear more . . . later.
Right now it looks like that bird
is thinking about his own
idea of chicken dinner—
us. So how about that
magic trick?"

The killer fowl started bobbing and walking toward us.

Fred bounced his fist off the top of my head. "Yeah, come on, Joe. You are the worst magician I've ever known. Your *Book* got us into this. Do a real magic trick for once and get us out of here."

The chicken started trotting.

I racked my brain. There was no way I was going to try the classic "abracadabra" or "hocus pocus" magic words to stop a charging chicken. And don't even remind me of that "please" and "thank you" mistake I made earlier in my career. But I had a flash of an idea. I thought it could work. It just might work. So I gave it a try.

"Why did the chicken cross the road?" I yelled.

The chicken only flapped its wings and ran faster.

I cupped my hands like a megaphone and yelled punch lines: "To get to the other side. To buy the newspaper. To get away from Colonel Sanders."

Nothing worked. The monster chicken just looked madder and ran at us faster.

"I don't want to end up as chicken feed," wailed Sam, plastered against the fence.

4

At that moment, I saw a sign out of the corner of my eye. And I knew where we were.

The chicken thundered toward us, its deadly sharp beak pointed directly at us.

I stepped in front of Sam and Fred with my chest out.

"Hoboken," I said.

"Chicken," said Fred.

"Emergency!" screamed Sam.

"Exactly."

# TWO

This is going to be impossible to explain. But give me a chance and just let me try. I think I know what happened.

To go back to the very beginning—my life has not been the same since my uncle Joe gave me *The Book* for my birthday. This book is a small book. A dark blue book with strange silver writing on it. A book like no book I've ever read before or since. It's a time-warping book.

I know. I know. I can hear you laughing right now. You're saying to yourself, "What's with this guy? He probably still believes in the Easter Bunny and the Tooth Fairy. Everybody knows you can't travel through time with a book."

I don't blame you for not believing. I didn't really believe it myself, either. Then we opened *The Book* and started going places.

Since then, my friends Sam and Fred and I have gotten into trouble in just about every time from the Stone Age to the future. We've run into pirates, robots, cavemen, you name it. We've been chased by a woolly mammoth, stampeded by cattle, turned into mummies, and nearly suffocated by one very nasty-smelling giant.

And we still have absolutely no idea how to work *The Book*.

The only thing that seems to stay the same is the green mist that takes us places. And that once we go to another time, the only way to get back home to our time is to find *The Book* in that time.

So anyway, there we were—sitting in my room

the very first day of summer vacation. We were trying to be careful. We really were.

Fred was sitting on my bed, putting new wheels on his skates, showing off his new Detroit Red Wings Stanley Cup Champions hat. Sam and I were at my desk.

"No more classes, no more books. No more teachers' dirty looks," chanted Fred.

Sam raised one eyebrow. "What a poet. You wouldn't know it. But your feet show it. They're Longfellows."

Fred looked up from his skates. "Hey, what's that supposed to mean . . . ?"

I stepped in between them before they started anything. "Okay guys. Forget the poetry. We are gathered here today to decide one great question: How do we spend our summer vacation?"

Sam raised his hand. "May I first suggest how we *don't* spend our summer vacation?" He pointed to a thin blue book with silver designs on my bookshelf. "Can we please promise not to open *The Book* and get sucked into some time-travel trouble like we always do when we get together?"

I started, "But—"

"No buts," said Sam. "Every time you figure out some new way to keep track of *The Book,* we just get in more trouble. Let's stay right here, right now."

"I'm with you," said Fred, spinning his wheels. "I say we do nothing but skate, skate, skate, and skate. We don't have to open any books."

"Well, now that you mention books," said Sam, "I was thinking we might get an early start on this list. Then we can do whatever we want for the rest of the summer."

Fred grabbed the piece of paper from Sam's hand and read the heading. "Summer reading list? Are you crazy? This is vacation. We don't have to read anything. That's why they call it vacation."

Sam took his list back. He read aloud, "Each student must read four books during the summer and fill out the attached study guide for two of them."

"How can you be thinking about books?" said Fred. "We've got skating moves to practice."

"Hmmm," said Sam. "The list has *Hatchet, The Phantom Tollbooth, The Hoboken Chicken Emergency* . . ."

Fred used the edge of my bed to practice his street skating moves. "We've got to perfect the unity, the mute grab, the backside royale . . ."

". . . *Matilda, Flat Stanley* . . ."

". . . gumby, stale Japan . . . "

Fred and Sam traded skate moves and book titles one-on-one.

". . . or here's *Tuck Everlasting* . . ."

". . . rocket three-sixty . . ."

". . . *Bunnicula* . . ."

". . . fishbrain . . ."

Without looking up from the list, Sam grabbed Fred's hat and tossed it on the floor.

"*Encyclopedia Brown.*"

Fred did a half-twist flip off the bed and took Sam's list. He stuck it in a book from my shelf, shoved the book back on the shelf, and jumped back onto the bed.

"Mistyflip."

"*George and Martha.*"

"One-eighty monkey plant."

"Guys—"

"*Frog and Toad.*"

"Alley-oop soul."

"*Forget it, you guys!*" I yelled. "You don't have to decide."

Fred and Sam both stopped and looked at me.

"What do you mean we don't have to decide?"

I pointed to my bookshelf.

"The way I figure it, we have about three seconds before this green mist leaking off my bookshelf decides for us."

All three of us stared at the wisps of green mist swirling out of the thin blue book with silver designs.

"Aww no," said Fred. "How did that happen? I didn't do nothing."

"Anything," said Sam. "You didn't do anything . . . except put our summer reading list inside *The Book*."

"So, what will that do?" asked Fred.

"We'll find out soon enough," I said.

Then the familiar green mist washed over us. And we were flung through time and space to who knows when or where.

# THREE

The chicken thundered toward us.

"Don't worry," I said, standing in front of Fred and Sam. "I know exactly what's going to happen next."

Sam crouched down and covered his head. "Yeah, death by chicken."

The galloping chicken was ten feet away and closing fast.

"Are you sure you know what's going to happen?" said Fred.

"*Yerrbbfff,*" said Sam's muffled voice.

The enormous chicken hopped, flapped, and launched itself right at us.

I thought I knew what was going to happen. I hoped I knew.

The feathered monster rose up . . . up . . . and . . . just over us. It cleared the fence behind us

13

with a foot to spare, and landed with a ground-shaking *thud*. The big bird gave one more "CLUCK" and then disappeared down the street.

Sam froze in his crouch. "I can't bear to look. Are we dead yet?"

"Yes," said Fred. "And I'm the ghost of Fred." Fred nudged Sam with one knee. Sam fell over, still curled in a ball. He carefully opened one eye.

"Fred, Joe—you're alive!" said Sam. "You're sideways, but you're alive!"

Fred rolled Sam back upright.

"Like magic," said Sam. "Now you're perfect." Sam got on his knees and bowed to me. "Joe the Magnificent, I take back all of the bad things I ever said about you. You are a genius. You did know what was going to happen."

"Well—" I began.

Sam wrapped his arms around my knees. "So you must know where *The Book* is and how we can get it and go back home and not stick around to fight giant chickens or slay dragons or wrestle pirates or—"

"Not exactly—" I began.

Fred hopped a handrail, practicing a backside royale. "What do you mean 'not exactly'? And

14

how did you know that chicken was going to jump?"

"That's what I've been trying to tell you," I said. "I saw that sign that says HOBOKEN DELI and I knew exactly where we were."

"Hoboken?" said Fred.

"Brilliant," said Sam.

"Well not exactly Hoboken," I said. "I saw Hoboken, then the chicken, and then Sam said 'emergency.'"

A look of understanding came across Sam's face. "No. This is not possible."

"It's exactly like this book I read," I went on. "*The Hoboken Chicken Emergency*. This kid lives in Hoboken. He gets a two-hundred-sixty-six-pound chicken for Thanksgiving. He takes it to a playground. Then it runs away and jumps over the fence."

Fred and Sam stared at me with their mouths hanging open.

"Are you telling me we are inside the book *The Hoboken Chicken Emergency* by D. Manus Pinkwater?" said Sam.

"It all fits," I said. "The playground. Hoboken. The two-hundred-sixty-six-pound chicken."

"We can't be in a book," said Fred. "That only happens in those geeky movies. Besides, there is no way I am going to spend my summer vacation in a book."

Sam slowly shook his head. "This is very weird, but quite possibly true. What if story characters are real in some way? What if they have a life we just don't know about?"

"That would explain everything," I said.

"Almost everything," said Fred, tugging nervously on his hat. "Everything except that frog in a suit coat and pants over there."

I looked around. "There's no frog in a suit in *The Hoboken Chicken Emergency*. Where?"

"Right there," pointed Fred. "Next to the toad in the plaid jacket."

"Frog?" I said.

"Toad?" Sam said.

We looked at each other in horror.

*"Frog and Toad?"* we said.

And we knew then and there that something had gone terribly, mixed-uply, summer-reading-listly wrong.

# FOUR

Fred, Sam, and I hung on the playground fence. We watched the human-size frog in a green suit coat and striped pants and the toad in a plaid coat turn the corner and run down the street.

"I saw it, but I don't believe it," I said.

"How did they get here?" asked Fred.

"The summer reading list was for the whole school," answered Sam. "First grade through eighth grade. *Green Eggs and Ham* through *20,000 Leagues Under the Sea*."

I shook my head. "But you don't really think all of those books...? I mean did we...? Are they...?"

Black clouds swept over the sun. A bolt of lightning flashed. Thunder cracked.

A rabbit in a blue coat with brass buttons, a curious-looking monkey, and a boy pushing a

18

wheelbarrow filled with one very large orange carrot ran toward us down the street.

Sam's eyes widened. "Quick, hide!" He pushed us under a bench behind a bush.

"Why are we hiding from Peter Rabbit?" whispered Fred.

Another flash of lightning split the dark Hoboken sky. The crack of thunder shook the ground under us. A giant figure with a bleached skull head and antlers galloped his black horse behind Peter.

I peeked through the slats of the bench and the leaves of the bushes. The antlered giant swung his sword overhead, then reined his horse to a stop. He turned his flaming eyes our way. I could have sworn he was staring right at us. My heart stopped. Just then, the monkey let out a shriek. The antler guy turned his head, then spurred his horse and rode off.

The black cloud passed. It took us a few minutes to get slowly to our feet and brush the dirt off our knees.

"Does that answer your question?" asked Sam.

Even Fred, who has stood up to Blackbeard the pirate, crocodiles on the Nile, and a twelve-foot vert wall half pipe, seemed shaken.

"Who . . . ? What . . . ?"

"That was the Horned King," said Sam. "One very nasty character from Lloyd Alexander's *The Book of Three*."

"Oh no," I said. "We are in huge trouble. If this means what I think it means, all of the characters from every book on the summer reading list are mixed up here in Hoboken. And none of them are in their books where they're supposed to be. The librarian is going to kill us."

Fred slapped me with his hat. "And I'm going to kill you if you blow my whole skating summer chasing Nancy Drew and Pippi Longstocking."

"I don't believe Nancy was on the list," said Sam.

Fred punched Sam. "You know what I mean."

"Knock it off, you guys," I said. "We've got to take care of this before things really go wrong. Like what if the Horned King makes Peter Rabbit stew?"

"What if the Red Queen says, 'Off with Ramona's head!'?" said Sam.

"What if the Twits mess up Wayside School?" I said.

"What if the Tripods take over the Little House on the Prairie?" said Sam.

"Now that might be a good thing," said Fred.

We both gave Fred a look.

"Aw, come on," said Fred. "You've got to admit it would make that book a lot more exciting."

"We've got to get everyone back in the right book," said Sam. "Otherwise it will just . . . just . . . be wrong."

I jumped up on the bench. "I know just what we have to do."

"Now you're even acting like somebody in one of those lame books," said Fred.

I pretended I didn't hear him and went on. "We

have to get back *The Book* and take the summer reading list out of it before anything permanent happens."

Sam sat on the bench. "Oh good. We have to find *The Book* to fix everything. That's original."

Fred slumped next to Sam. "We need Sherlock Holmes or somebody. Where are we going to find *The Book*?"

I looked up, trying to figure out where we should look . . . and I saw the answer. "There," I said, pointing to a spiderweb in the corner of the fence. "The answer is right there over your head."

# FIVE

Fred and Sam turned to look where I was pointing. We all stared in amazement at the spiderweb. Because there in the center of the web, neatly woven in block letters, was a message. It said:

THE

LIBRARY

We all went weak in the knees. Things were getting stranger by the minute.

"It's Charlotte," whispered Sam.

"The librarian?" said Fred.

"No, you doofus," said Sam. "The spider. Didn't you ever read *Charlotte's Web?*"

"Uh . . . yeah. Sure I did," said Fred. "I must have just missed that Charlotte part."

"She's in the whole book," said Sam. "She spins messages in her web to save the pig."

"Right," said Fred. "I knew that."

"Of course," I said. "Where else would *The Book* be? The library."

"So what are we waiting for?" said Fred. "Let's get to the library, check out *The Book,* and get home to skate."

"There is just one small problem," said Sam, adjusting his glasses like he always does when he knows something we don't know. "We have absolutely no idea where the Hoboken Library is."

The three of us sat back down on the bench. We could waste the whole day looking for the library. By then it might be too late to save Frog and Toad and Peter Rabbit and who knows who else. I glanced up at Charlotte's web again.

"Oh yes we do," I said. Because there in the center of the web, neatly woven in block letters was a message. It said:

500 PARK AVE.
6 BLOCKS WEST ON 5TH STREET
ACROSS FROM
CHURCH SQUARE PARK
M, T, TH: 9–8
W, F: 9–5
SAT: 11–2
CLOSED SUNDAY

24

We took off west on Fifth Street. We passed old houses, an alley, a street lined with delis, bars, and shops. In just a few minutes we were at the corner of the park.

I looked around the deserted streets. "Does something seem weird to you?"

"Oh no," said Sam. "I get sucked into a book and walk around inside it every day. Of course this seems weird."

"No, I mean how come there are no people walking around?"

"Hey, yeah," said Fred. "It's like that *Twilight Zone* episode where the guy can stop and start time with a watch. But he breaks the watch while everyone is frozen and he's the only one left and he goes crazy and starts screaming and crying and—"

"Thanks for that cheerful little story," said Sam. "But I think we're not in the real Hoboken. We're in the Hoboken from the book. Only characters from the book are here. So—"

Just then we heard a wild yelling and the sound of stomping footsteps behind us. Fred, Sam, and I ran into the park and dove behind a statue with a big base.

Two large gray hippos ran down the street on

their hind legs. One wore a red striped dress and a flower behind her ear. The other had one gold tooth.

"Hold the course or I'll keelhaul the both of ye," growled a strangely dressed guy. He hopped along on one leg and a crutch. A parrot perched on his shoulder. He fired a shot from a huge pistol over the hippos' heads.

"Pieces of eight, pieces of eight," squawked the parrot.

The one-legged pirate chased the hippos up the steps and between the two big columns of an old brick building. Then everything went quiet again.

We sat down behind the statue and looked at each other. We've seen some strange things in our time-warp travels together, but nothing as strange as this.

Sam wiped his glasses with his shirt. "George and Martha?"

"Chased by Long John Silver?" said Fred.

I peeked around the statue to take another look and saw a stranger sight times ten. I saw Homer Price being carried by the Headless Horseman. Dracula was dragging Winnie-the-Pooh in a head-lock. Mr. Twit was breaking Harold's purple cray-

on. I saw twenty different bad guys from twenty different books chasing, hauling, and pushing all kinds of characters up the steps of the big old brick building. And just when I thought things couldn't get any stranger, I saw a sight that froze my blood.

I sat back down behind the statue. I didn't have the heart to tell Sam and Fred.

"What was it?" said Sam. "You look like you've seen a ghost. Is it Frankenstein? Moby Dick? How bad could it be? The Babysitters' Club?"

I could only motion weakly and point to the big brick building.

Sam looked around the statue and collapsed next to me. "No . . ."

Fred looked at the two of us. "What? What is it?"

Sam and I pointed. Fred looked out and read the sign on the big brick building. The building every bad character from the summer reading list was heading into.

Fred read the sign out loud: "Hoboken Public Library." Then he collapsed next to us.

# SIX

"That's it. We're cooked," said Sam.

I tried to think of a plan or even a magic trick to use. But I couldn't.

"Things could be worse," I said.

"Things could be worse?" squeaked Sam. "Things could be worse?" He was starting to look a little hysterical. "The one building in Hoboken that we need to get into is filled with monsters, criminals, and killers. It's packed with every bad guy from every book ever written. We have to sneak in and find one small book in the middle of thousands of library books. And all you can say is, 'Things could be worse'?"

Sam's hair sprouted out in every direction. His glasses hung crookedly. Now he was definitely hysterical.

"Well," said Fred calmly, "we could be captured

and getting dragged in there like everybody else. That would be worse."

Sam stared at Fred like he was going to strangle him.

I stared at Fred like I was going to hug him.

"Fred," I said. "You are a genius. That's exactly how we'll get in there. We don't even need a magic trick. You pretend to be a bad guy character from a book who captures us. You chase us into the library."

"I what?" said Fred. "I am? Okay."

Sam wasn't too thrilled with the plan. But even he had to admit we didn't have much choice. We had to get into the library as soon as we could and get our hands on *The Book*.

Fred turned his Red Wings hat backward and rolled his sleeves up over his shoulders to look as nasty as possible. Sam and I combed our hair down to look as nerdy as possible.

Fred, Sam, and I checked each other out. Fred pulled his belt out of his pants.

"Ready?" I asked.

"Ready," said Sam and Fred.

"Then let's go."

Sam and I jumped out from behind the statue and headed for the library. Fred ran behind us, yelling and whipping his belt around. "That's it. Keep moving, you chuckleheads." He landed a solid belt whip on Sam's leg.

"Hey!" said Sam. "That hurts."

"And there's more where that came from," yelled Fred, chasing us up the library steps. "So don't give me any grief, four eyes."

We pushed through the front doors and right into one incredibly ugly troll and a gangster guarding the next doors. The troll had a crazy look in his eye. The gang- ster had a machine gun.

"Who's that crossing my bridge?" said the troll.

"Yeah. Who are you mugs? And what patty- cake book did you fall out of?" said the gang- ster, chewing his cigar.

I smoothed my hair and straightened my collar. "We are

31

the Time Warp Trio," I said in my best nerd voice. "Sam and I do good deeds and help people wherever we go. But Fred is the mean kid next door. He always wrecks our plans."

"Time Warp Trio?" said the gangster. "I didn't never hear of no books called the Time Warp Trio. Whaddayou, some kinda science fiction or somethin'?"

The troll hiccupped and drooled a pool of yellowish saliva on his green hairy foot.

"Nah, we're like action adventure fiction," said Fred. "These jerks try to make them educational adventures. I make sure to mess 'em up and keep things moving so the readers don't fall asleep." Fred gave Sam and me a smack on the back of our heads.

The gangster pointed his machine gun at us and gave us a cold stare. Sam and I thought we were goners. He chewed his cigar, then broke into a laugh.

"Hey, dat's funny. You sound like my kinda guy. Reminds me of stories I was in when I was a kid."

Fred smiled and gave us an extra couple of slaps Sam and I didn't think were really necessary.

"Take 'em inside." The gangster motioned with

his machine gun. "The Boss has plans for characters like them."

The troll's stomach rumbled. He burped, and another string of drool spilled down his chin.

Fred grabbed Sam and me by the backs of the necks and pushed us quickly through the doors before the gangster changed his mind. The three of us stumbled into the library and stopped dead.

You know how when you read a book you kind of "see" the characters even if they don't show a picture of them? Well, that's what this was like. But instead of seeing book characters in our minds, we saw them for real, wandering all over the Hoboken Public Library, characters from every book on our summer reading list.

"I see it, but I don't believe it," whispered Sam. "That's Mrs. Twit tying up Mary Poppins and Encyclopedia Brown."

"That's Frankenstein holding Pippi Longstocking," I breathed.

"They even got Mother Goose," said Fred.

I could just see Peter Rabbit, Henrietta the 266-pound Hoboken chicken, George and Martha, and ten or twenty other characters already trapped in a kind of cage made out of library shelves behind the main desk. Huge stacks of books towered over them.

"There's that girl with the yellow hat who has her appendix taken out," I said.

"Madeline," said Sam.

"And that vampire rabbit we read about last year," said Fred.

"Bunnicula," said Sam. "And Flat Stanley, Treehorn, Alice in Wonderland, Nate the Great, Amelia Bedelia . . . they're all here," said Sam in amazement.

We couldn't see who "the Boss" was. He was running things from the main checkout desk, completely surrounded by some very bad-looking characters.

"Keelhaul the lot of them," boomed Long John Silver.

"Off with their heads," commanded the Red Queen.

"Kill the pig! Cut his throat! Bash him in!" chanted a scrawny kid dressed in ripped clothes with streaks of mud, pounding his pointed stick spear on a library table.

"I don't know what's going on here, but it doesn't look good," I said. "Let's sneak up those stairs and start looking for *The Book*—quick."

And it probably would have been a good plan. But we were only halfway up the stairs when we heard a voice that could only be talking to us.

"You three boys. What book are you from? Come down here now."

I turned to see who had spotted us. I had to blink to make sure I wasn't seeing things. Because standing between the White Witch from Narnia and The Trunchbull from *Matilda* was a little red man pointing his finger directly at us.

"This does not look good," I said.

"This looks positively evil," said Sam.

"Is that who I think it is?" said Fred.

I thought about it for a second. "Do you know any other red guy with two horns and a pointed tail?"

# SEVEN

The Devil motioned us back down to the main desk.

We had no choice but to go.

We walked down the steps and across the floor covered with the books that had been thrown everywhere. Characters from all kinds of stories milled around.

We stepped over a very hungry caterpillar eating his way through a dictionary. We pushed past a mother duck and her line of ducklings. We made our way through a crowd made up of Robinson Crusoe, a blue moose, Julie with some wolves, a snowman, a plain and tall lady named Sarah, a kid with a hatchet, and a very confused-looking Robin Hood helping Eeyore reattach his tail.

We stood in front of the horned guy, speechless.

So this was "the Boss" behind this terrible scene.

The Devil sat in the librarian's chair surrounded by outlaws, Wild Things, and a lot of generally bad-looking characters. He looked us over, twirling the little beard on his chin. He checked a list on his clipboard.

"And you are—?"

"Uh . . . Joe, Sam, and Fred," I said.

"And from which book might that be?"

I panicked. I knew the Devil probably wouldn't believe the same weak story we told those not-too-bright guards at the front door. So I decided to just pretend our real lives were a story. They were definitely weird enough to sound like fiction.

"We're the Time Warp Trio," I said. "We travel around in time and have adventures and stuff."

The Devil pulled at his beard while he checked his alphabetical list. "I have a *Time Cat,* a *Time of Wonder,* and then *A Toad for Tuesday.* But no *Time Warp Trio.*"

"Off with their heads!" yelled the Red Queen.

The Devil looked up and looked right through me. "Do you know your author?"

That threw me for a loop. "Um . . . sure . . . I mean no . . . I mean I'm not sure . . . I think it starts with an *s* . . . maybe. . . ?" I started making up any answer I could think of.

Sam saw I was in trouble and jumped in to help. "We go a lot of different places. So each adventure has a different title. We're probably not under 'Time Warp Trio' because we're actually a series."

Frankenstein gave a mad groan: "Series—bad!" and made a move to wring our necks. The Devil held him back.

"No, no. Settle down your goose bumps, Frank. They're not from one of those horror series. They look more like kids who would travel around on a magic school bus or something."

"Hey, no way," said Fred, stepping up to the desk and getting into it. "Joe does some unreal magic tricks. Sam is *the* joke-and-riddle brainiac. And I usually save the day with my mad skills."

The Devil looked completely confused.

"Mad skills!" squawked the parrot. "Mad skills!"

"Shiver my timbers," boomed Long John Silver. "He's not even speaking the King's English. Clap him in irons with the rest of them!"

The Devil tapped his pencil on his list. "I'm not quite sure what you said, young man. But maybe you can make this easier on all of us. What we are doing here is separating the good characters from the bad characters. The bad characters stay here and take over any story they like. . . ."

He motioned to the bogeymen, goblins, and people who cut in front of you in the lunch line.

"And the good characters go there . . ."

He motioned to the characters behind him.

". . . to be crushed by those huge stacks of books and wiped out of stories forever."

The bad characters cheered and hooted and howled. The Devil smiled.

"So—are you good characters . . . or bad characters?"

Now I know it's wrong to lie. But I was still trying to figure out if it would be all that wrong to lie to the Devil . . . when Fred solved the problem.

"Oh, we're definitely bad," said Fred. "Watch this." He jumped on top of a library table, spun 570 degrees through the air to land backward on the stair's handrail, then slid down the whole rail fakie stale Japan on his shoes. "Now *that's* bad."

The Horned King nodded his big antlered head.

"And see this book?" I lifted a telephone-book-size volume called *Best Children's Books*. I grabbed a piece of string off the desk. I put the string through the middle of the book, closed it, and tied a knot at the back of the spine. I held the two ends of the string out. "I bet your baddest, strongest character can't pull the string so it's straight horizontally."

Jack's giant stepped up and grabbed the string. He pulled. The string stayed bowed. Frankenstein pulled. The string stayed bowed. The Cyclops

pulled and pulled and nearly popped his one eye out of his head. The string stayed bowed.

"That's bad," said a wolf in sheep's clothing.

"What building has the most stories?" said Sam.

"The Empire State Building?" guessed the Sheriff of Nottingham.

"No, the library," said Sam. "Where does Thursday come before Wednesday?"

From the captured good guys came a voice. "On a deserted island?" guessed Robinson Crusoe's Friday.

"No, the dictionary," said Sam. "What would

happen if you threw this yellow book into the Red Sea?"

"It would turn pink?" guessed one of the evil stepmothers.

"It would get wet," said Sam.

Everyone groaned.

"Stop, stop," said the Devil. "That is really bad."

All of the bad characters laughed and gathered around us. Fred showed the Horned King a half cab topside grind. Dracula and Sam traded vampire riddles. I was explaining some more impossible tricks to an evil scientist.

We were in. All we had to do was get our hands on *The Book,* and everything and everyone would be back where they belonged. Fred, Sam, and I smiled at each other.

Then the door with LIBRARIAN written on the glass slammed open with a bang.

"What is going on out here?!"

Injun Joe and Captain Ahab tried to hide behind a shelf. Everyone else became instantly quiet. All the nasty, murdering, cutthroat, bad characters in the place were standing looking nervously at their feet.

"Nothing, Boss," said the Devil.

We looked from the Devil to the fuzzy brown figure he was talking to. Then we knew we were in even weirder and bigger trouble.

"The Boss?" said Fred.

"A . . . a . . . teddy bear?" said Sam.

# EIGHT

"That's *Mr.* Bear to you, kid," growled the soft fuzzy teddy bear with a red ribbon around his neck.

We must have looked more than a little shocked. We didn't say anything else. But the teddy bear went crazy on us.

"This is exactly what I'm talking about. Just because I'm a teddy bear, I get no respect. Everyone thinks I'm soft and huggable and *stupid!*"

"Hey, we didn't say anything like that," said Fred.

Teddy Bear hopped up on the desk. "No, but I know what you're thinking. And that's all going to change."

Teddy Bear turned around and faced the Devil. "And what exactly is the holdup here? Why isn't everyone being crushed?"

The Devil shuffled his papers and pointed to us. "We were . . . uh . . . I was just . . . checking in these three characters."

Teddy Bear jumped off the desk and touched the ground. "Characters? Hah! That's a good one. They aren't characters from a book. These are three kids. Any moron can see that!"

"Any moron can see that!" screeched Long John's parrot.

Teddy Bear was really fuming now. "In fact, they are just the kind of readers I get no respect from—wise-guy boys." He shook his cute pudgy little paw at us. "Don't think I don't know your type. Nothing but action books, sports books, and nonfiction. Well, I'll give you some action. Throw them in the crusher *now!*"

A giant octopus wrapped its monster tentacles around us, tightly.

"Where the heck did that come from?" gasped Fred.

"20,000 *Leagues Under the Sea* would be my guess," wheezed Sam. "Probably eighth-grade list."

Getting yelled at by a teddy bear was bad enough. But being crushed by books and attacked by a character that wasn't even on our grade's reading list was just too much for me. I snapped.

"Now just one minute!" I screamed. I surprised even myself with how loud I yelled. Everyone stared. The octopus loosened its grip. I saw this was my one chance to save us from the horrible fate of getting flattened by hundreds of books. I decided to try reasoning with the teddy bear.

"Now look, Mr. Teddy—I mean Mr. Bear," I said. "It is probably true that we are not the biggest fans of teddy bear books."

"See! See! I told you. I told you," squealed Teddy Bear, spinning around.

"But crushing all of the good characters from every other book is not going to solve anything," I went on. (I tried my best to sound like my mom and dad when they're telling me what to do, but want me to think I have a choice.) "Just look how dumb these books sound without their main characters."

I bent over the tentacle around my waist and picked a book off the floor. "Look at this. Now *The Hoboken Chicken Emergency* is just *The Emergency*."

Fred picked up another book. "*Sylvester and the Magic Pebble* is *And the Magic Pebble*."

Sam picked up *The Gingerbread Man*. "There are giant holes in every story." He read:

"'Run run run,
as fast as you can.
You can't catch me,
I'm the blankety blank'?"

Teddy Bear looked at us with his big shining eyes. "Aww, that is so sweet. You are worried about all of the poor little books. Well, don't worry. Because the new titles of those books will be

*The Teddy Bear Emergency, Teddy Bear and the Magic Pebble,* and *The Teddy Bear Man!*"

He raised both fuzzy brown arms in the air and laughed a crazy hyper laugh at the ceiling. He kept laughing and babbling. "And then there will be *Encyclopedia Teddy Bear, Curious Mr. Twit, Bridge to Long John Silver . . .*"

His voice got higher and louder.

*"Frankenstein in Wonderland . . ."*

The bad characters cheered each new title.

*"The Devil in the Willows, Green Eggs and Dracula . . ."*

He was totally loony.

*"Headless-Horseman-the-Pooh, Teddy Bear Everlasting!* We're taking over!"

The bad characters gave a huge cheer. "Ted-dy! Ted-dy! Ted-dy!"

Teddy Bear ran around in little circles with his fuzzy arms raised.

The octopus tossed us into the cage with the good characters and slammed the metal bar door behind us. Fred, Sam, and I bounced off George, Martha, and Ramona. We lay on our backs looking up at the hundreds of books that were about to come crashing down on us.

50

This is it, I thought. The minute that twisted little bear gives the word, we will be flattened proof of what some kids have always suspected—reading can kill you.

I heard a voice. The books teetered. I closed my eyes.

It was too late to even scream.

# NINE

I heard the voice again. It didn't sound like Teddy Bear's voice.

I opened my eyes to see if we were still alive. Sam sat squeezed between George and Martha. Fred held Peter Rabbit in one arm and Ping in the other. I let out one long sigh of relief and looked at the front desk.

A girl about our age stood in front of Teddy Bear and his bad character pals.

"What the boys said makes sense."

Teddy Bear stared at the girl in amazement.

Long John Silver stared at her like she was a piece of steak about to be thrown to a hungry lion.

"If we're not in our books, who will tell all of the stories? Of how we crossed the river. How we cleared the land. How we cut the trees. Making the logs. Cutting a notch in the—"

"Okay already," said Teddy Bear. "Could you speed it up? I'm just about to knock over these books and crush these characters out of existence."

"Who the heck is she?" whispered Fred.

"I think it's that girl who lived on the prairie," said Sam.

We all shivered, remembering that required-reading book.

"Then there was the time I accidentally poured the currant wine at tea," said the girl. "I was only looking for raspberry cordial and I had so wanted to use the rosebud tea set but of course that was never used except for the minister . . ."

"Or maybe she's Anne of Green Gables," whispered Sam.

"I see—" began Teddy Bear. But the girl kept going.

"And then that Christmas without Father was so lonely yet so splendid because Father was away as a chaplain and Meg and Jo and Amy and Marmee . . ."

"Yes—" began Teddy Bear. But the girl kept going.

"One of the Little Women?" I guessed.

"Or the time I took trick riding because who

knew when it might come in handy when I had a mystery to solve, and sure enough, later that week . . ."

Teddy Bear sat down and started listening.

"Nancy Drew?" guessed Fred. The girl kept going.

". . . after that summer, babysitting was never the same. The club met over at my house . . ."

The Devil propped his chin in his hand to keep his head up.

"Babysitters' Club?" I guessed.

". . . and I knew Annie had beauty, talent, and the drive to be a cheerleader. But I was not about to let her ruin the reputation of our squad . . ."

"Definitely Sweet Valley High," I said.

Somebody yawned. Sam nudged me in the ribs and pointed to Frankenstein. He was struggling mightily to keep his eyelids open. First one eye would close. Then the other. Both eyes popped open. They closed.

". . . we passed notes in school by curling up the piece of paper, slipping it in the iron scroll of the desk . . ."

The Headless Horseman and the Horned King sat propped up against each other. No one could see their eyes. But neither one of them was moving anymore. Long John Silver let out a soft little snore.

"Betty?" guessed Fred. "Veronica?"

"American Girls?" I guessed.

"That's it," whispered Sam.

"Who's it?"

"She's all of those girls," said Sam. "We never read any of those books. So we couldn't tell one character from another if we had to. She's all of those girl characters rolled into one!"

"Now *that's* scary," said Fred.

Teddy Bear leaned forward, looking at the Girl through half-closed eyes. The Red Queen had long since laid her head on the table. Dracula was wrapped in sweet dreams in his cape. Teddy Bear was the last bad character still awake.

". . . Pa didn't have no nails. But he said a man don't need no nails to make a door. This is how he did it. . . ."

Teddy Bear closed one eye and leaned against the sleeping Devil.

". . . and when you are filled with sadness and in the depths of despair, doesn't it just feel like a lump of caramel in your throat . . ."

Teddy Bear's last open eye winked . . . half closed . . . and then dropped shut. His chin fell forward on his chest. And he snored the biggest growling snore of any of the fast-asleep bad guys.

I put my finger to my lips. Fred slowly and care-

fully swung open the metal door. Sam led everyone out from under the stack of books teetering above us. Martha carried Piglet. Pooh cradled Peter Rabbit.

". . . 'It takes time to develop a good relationship,' I told Annie . . ."

The Hoboken Chicken tiptoed carefully through the sleeping octopus's tentacles. Madeline stepped over Mr. McGregor's hoe. Fred slipped Flat Stanley between the doors so he could unlock them. Harold, Nate, Pippi, and all the others snuck outside into the sunshine and freedom.

Robin Hood led the last of the kids from Wayside School between the sleeping gangster and the still-drooling troll.

Fred and I stood in the doorway and looked back.

". . . a suspicious character threw a rock. My horse reared almost straight up . . ."

Fred and I looked at each other. We looked back at the Girl who had saved us and all of the characters.

". . . for Christmas in Sweden, one girl in each family would get to dress in a long white dress and red sash with a crown of green leaves and lighted candles . . ."

Fred headed outside. I grabbed him by the arm and dragged him back. We picked the Girl up by each elbow and carried her, still talking, carefully toward the library door.

". . . and what a secret it was! Just three words I whispered in his ear . . ."

We were just at the foot of the stairs when I saw, out of the corner of my eye, a flutter of motion near Long John Silver.

". . . next Pa cut a wide deep notch near the edge—"

"*Bbbwwwaaauuukk!*" squawked Long John's parrot. "Near the edge! Near the edge!"

Teddy Bear's eyes popped open. The eyes of every bad character in the library popped open. Teddy Bear saw the now-empty room. Teddy Bear saw Fred and me carrying the Girl.

He screamed in a not-very-cuddly voice, "Crush those boys *now!*"

# TEN

**M**r. McGregor swung his hoe. The Horned King drew his sword.

"We'll never make it to the door," said Fred. "Quick. Up these stairs."

We charged up the steps two at a time with the Girl leading the way. Captain Ahab and a snake-haired woman climbed after us. The Devil and a red-golden dragon scrambled right behind them.

We reached the top landing, blocked by the stack of books that had been meant to crush us. I had a brainstorm. "Get back here and push!"

The Girl and Fred climbed around behind the books with me. We pushed and pushed and toppled an avalanche of dusty old books down the stairs. I saw the Red Queen disappear under a full set of Funk and Wagnall's encyclopedias. Mrs. Twit took a four-volume *History of the Civil War* right on her chin. Her glass eye popped out, and she flipped over the handrail. A beautiful blue *Historical Atlas of the World* flattened the Headless Horseman.

But a whole new wave of bad characters swarmed over the fallen books.

This time it was the Girl who came up with the brainstorm.

"Come on, boys. Use our only weapon," she called. And she machine-gunned a whole row of Hardy Boys books off one end of a shelf onto the Cyclops' head.

"Nice shot," said Fred. He knocked out a goblin with a rapid-fire set of American Girls. "Don't you love a good series?"

Then we hit them with the heavy artillery. I tossed *The Complete Illustrated Book of All Animals*. Fred chucked *Big Paintings by Everyone Who Ever Did One*. The Girl unloaded *The Big Big Big Dictionary of Names*.

Teddy Bear screamed, "You are making me angry!" and shook his soft fuzzy paw at us.

I knew he was right. And I knew we couldn't hold out for much longer. I looked around for a way to escape. Stairs blocked. Windows too high to reach. Books piled on the other side. That's when I saw our salvation.

Because there, across the lobby, in the piles of books stacked over the desk, in between *Hot Men of Science* and *You and Your Koala Bear*, sat a thin blue book covered with silver stars and moons along the back. A folded list stuck out of the middle of it.

"*The Book!*" I yelled.

"Where?" said Fred.

Surrounded by books, the Girl looked at us like we were crazy.

As I pointed across the room at *The Book*, I suddenly and sadly realized we were no better off than we had been before. There was no way to get to

*The Book* without going down the stairs, through a pack of very mad characters we had just conked with some very heavy books, and back up over the desk where Teddy Bear was at this moment throwing a screaming tantrum.

"I will squash you! I will flatten you like the bugs you are!" yelled Teddy Bear. "No one ruins my plans. I will be the most famous character in every story!"

"Why do you need that book?" asked the Girl.

"It's magic enough to get everyone out of here and back into their own books," I said. "But forget it. There is no way we can get there from here."

I figured we were doomed to meet a messy and bookish end at the hands of a crazed teddy bear. I looked over at Fred. And when I saw that look in his eye, and saw him measuring lines and distances, I knew he figured differently.

"Give me some cover," said Fred. "I think a one-eighty monkey plant to an alley-oop fishbrain into a mistyflip rocket air should get me just high enough for a one-handed book grab."

I looked down at the swarming bad guys, then looked back at Fred. "Are you crazy? This isn't a kung-fu skate movie. As soon as those guys see what you're up to, they'll be all over you."

"That's why I need you to keep pelting them with books," said Fred.

"Do you think you can make it?" asked the Girl.

Fred looked over his route once more. He pulled his Red Wings cap low, then nodded.

"So what are you waiting for?" She let out a wild whoop and started firing every book she could get her hands on at the nasty gang below. I gave a yell and started winging books, too.

Fred jumped the handrail and slid halfway down before anyone figured out what was happening. Long John Silver stood up to swing his crutch, but I took him out with volume 7 of *Junior Classics: Legends of Long Ago*. Fred hit the end of the rail, launched a perfect mistyflip over the Devil's horns, and rocketed up toward *The Book*.

"Stop that boy!" screamed Teddy Bear.

Now I don't know if everything really slowed down like it always does in those kung-fu action movies. But it sure looked like it to me.

Fred's hand rose to *The Book*. So did Long John's parrot. Fred's hand. The parrot's beak. Both closed on *The Book* at the same instant. Fred pulled. The parrot pulled. Fred, *The Book,* the parrot . . .

And that's when the Girl tomahawked volume 2 of *Junior Classics: Once upon a Time* through the air. It smacked the parrot and popped it off *The Book* with a loud squawk and a puff of green feathers.

Fred bobbled *The Book,* pulled the summer reading list out, and then fell into the pileup of Teddy Bear, Devil, Red Queen, White Witch, and Horned King below.

The Girl and I looked at each other for one horrified second. We thought Fred was history.

Then I saw the wisp of pale green smoke rising from the pile of characters. The wisp turned into a stream. The stream turned into a twisting river. And the river turned into a whirling tornado of pale green mist that sucked up every character and book inside and outside the Hoboken Public Library.

I had just enough time to give the Girl a wave of thanks . . . and we were gone.

# ELEVEN

Fred landed on top of my desk, surrounded by the pileup of books that had been blown off my shelves. In one hand he held *The Book*. In the other hand he held the summer reading list.

I lay on my bed, still feeling a little time-warp queasy.

Sam was nowhere to be seen.

"Oh no," I said. "Sam was outside with the other characters when the mist scooped us up."

"He must still be in Hoboken," said Fred, jumping down off the desk.

I looked at the pile of books and had a terrible thought. "Or sucked into some other book," I said.

Fred and I attacked the books, flipping through all of them, looking for Sam.

"Here's the Hoboken Chicken," I said. "She made it back into her book."

"The Twits are both here," said Fred.

"Mary Poppins, Charlotte, Frog and Toad—everybody's back. Sam!" I yelled at the pile of books. "Where are you?"

We heard a very faint noise. It sounded like Sam's voice.

"Are you in *The White Mountains*?" called Fred, flipping it open.

"Are you in *Treasure Island*?" I called, leafing through it.

"Help!" came a muffled cry. It was definitely Sam's voice.

"Hang on, Sam," said Fred. "We'll get you out."

We flipped through *Winnie-the-Pooh*, *The BFG*, *Fat Men from Space*, and *Treehorn Times Three*. Still no Sam.

That's when Fred and I both spotted the scariest book on the desk. We saw it, but couldn't bring ourselves to pick it up. It was *Little House on the Prairie*.

"Help! Help! Help!" yelled Sam's muffled voice.

"Oh no," said Fred. "What if we can't get him out? What if he's stuck in there forever?" Fred carefully picked up *Little House on the Prairie* between one finger and thumb.

I took it carefully, breathed a deep breath . . . and opened it.

Sam came tumbling out of my closet, fighting my shirts, pants, and hangers wrapped around him.

Fred and I took one look and fell back laughing. Sam finally pulled my basketball shorts off his head. He stood there still covered in clothes and hangers. We started laughing all over again.

"Ahem."

We froze.

"Ahem."

It was my little sister Anna, standing in the doorway.

"I don't really want to know what you are doing," said Anna. "I just wanted to ask you, Joe, if you have any ribbon I can use for my—"

Anna held out her stuffed toy. And before

the words "teddy bear" were even out of her mouth, the three of us dove into my closet screaming, "Nooooooo!"

Anna backed slowly out of my room. She held her teddy bear behind her. We peeked out of the closet.

"You guys are so weird," said Anna. "So weird."

# Summer Reading List

Each student must read four books during the summer and fill out the attached study guide for two of them.

### EARLY READERS

*Amelia Bedelia* (series), by Peggy Parish

*The Carrot Seed,* by Ruth Krauss

*The Cat in the Hat,* by Dr. Seuss

*Curious George* (series), by H. A. Rey

*Frog and Toad* (series), by Arnold Lobel

*George and Martha* (series), by James Marshall

*Green Eggs and Ham,* by Dr. Seuss

*Grimms Fairy Tales*

*Harold and the Purple Crayon,* by Crockett Johnson

*The House at Pooh Corner,* by A. A. Milne

*Madeline* (series), by Ludwig Bemelmans

*Make Way for Ducklings,* by Robert McCloskey

*Mother Goose*

*Nate the Great* (series), by Marjorie W. Sharmat

*The Snowman,* by Raymond Briggs

*The Story About Ping,* by Marjorie Flack

*Sylvester and the Magic Pebble,* by William Steig

*The Tale of Peter Rabbit,* by Beatrix Potter
*The Three Billy Goats Gruff,* folk tale
*The Very Hungry Caterpillar,* by Eric Carle

## MIDDLE READERS

*Blue Moose, Fat Men from Space, The Hoboken Chicken Emergency,* and pretty much anything written by Daniel Manus Pinkwater
*Bunnicula,* by James Howe
*Charlotte's Web,* by E. B. White
*The Devil's Storybook,* by Natalie Babbitt
*Encyclopedia Brown* (series), by Donald J. Sobol
*Flat Stanley,* by Jeff Brown
*Hatchet,* by Gary Paulsen
*Homer Price,* by Robert McCloskey
*I Was a Teenage Gangster,* by A Badguy
*The Lion, the Witch, and the Wardrobe,* by C. S. Lewis
*Little House on the Prairie,* by Laura Ingalls Wilder
*Mary Poppins,* by P. L. Travers
*Pippi Longstocking,* by Astrid Lindgren
*Ramona* (series), by Beverly Cleary
*Robin Hood,* retold by Rosemary Sutcliff
*Sarah, Plain and Tall,* by Patricia MacLachlan
*Treehorn Times Three,* by Florence Parry Heide

*The Twits, Matilda, The BFG,* and a lot of things
by Roald Dahl
*Wayside School Is Falling Down,* by Louis Sachar
*The White Mountains,* by John Christopher
*The Wind in the Willows,* by Kenneth Grahame

OLDER READERS

*Adventures of Tom Sawyer,* by Mark Twain
*Aesop's Fables,* by Aesop
*Alice in Wonderland,* by Lewis Carroll
*The Book of Three,* and everything written by
Lloyd Alexander
*Bridge to Terabithia,* by Katherine Paterson
*Dracula,* by Bram Stoker
*Frankenstein,* by Mary Shelley
*Gods, Heroes and Men of Ancient Greece,* by
W. H. D. Rouse
*The Hobbit,* by J. R. R. Tolkien
*Julie of the Wolves,* by Jean Craighead George
*The Legend of Sleepy Hollow,* by Washington
Irving
*Lord of the Flies,* by William Golding
*Moby Dick,* by Herman Melville
*Robinson Crusoe,* by Daniel Defoe
*Treasure Island,* by Robert Louis Stevenson

*Tuck Everlasting,* by Natalie Babbitt
*Johnny Tremain,* by Esther Forbes
*20,000 Leagues Under the Sea,* by Jules Verne

BE-EXTREMELY-CAREFUL-WHEN-YOU-READERS
*Anything with Teddy Bears in It,* by Anyone

PERFECT-FOR-KNOCKING-OUT-PARROTS-AND-SAVING-
THE-DAY READERS
*Junior Classics, Volume Two: Once upon a Time*

STUDY GUIDE
- Write the title and author of the book.
- Identify two major characters of the book.
- Imagine who you would have play the major characters in the movie version of the book.
- Tap your pencil on the paper.
- Stare out the window and daydream.
- Put the study guide away and don't look at it again until the night before the first day of school.